CINDERS

ANNALEE ADAMS

CINDERS

First edition. October 2024.

ISBN: 9798343219807

This book has been typeset in Garamond.
www.AnnaleeAdams.biz

"I smiled, —for what had I

to fear?"

Edgar Allen Poe

1

As dark as night, as plain as day, I saw her. But she couldn't see me, though. Not with her gouged out eye or the wiry silver hair. She never even heard us coming. Her ear had been chopped off a long time ago. I shuddered. What happened to her? Maybe it's all part of the show? I stood still, watching her, taking in her flimsy frame as she sat outside the entrance to the fucked up Freak Show the boys wanted to go in. Were they mad? If the living corpse that guarded the entrance was anything to go by, the whole place would be a mangled mess of limbs and carnage. Which, of course, made my boyfriend's eyes light up like the fairground lights all around us.

"Come on Mollykins", he whined, using his

favourite pet name for me, which he knew I could never resist.

I huffed and took a step towards the looming entrance. It reminded me of the fireplace in the old Beetlejuice film my mum made me watch years ago; crooked and creepy. There was something dark about the place, a vibe that itched beneath my skin.

"Are you guys coming?" Leah yelled, giggling as John tickled her, pushing her through the curtained entrance.

"Hold up," Danny yelled, grabbing my hand and pulling me. I pulled against him. This place gave me the creeps more than that haunted rollercoaster at the theme park last year. He'd talked me into going for my sweet sixteenth. "Hey," he said, turning around. "It's all make up Mollykins, you'll see."

I nodded, biting my lip, and as I walked towards the entrance, the old woman moved in the chair and looked at me with her one remaining eye. I stopped dead in my tracks and she shook her head no.

"Huh?" I said.

"It's fine," Danny said. "She's playing on your fear. It's all part of the fun."

Fun? This wasn't my idea of fun! Bring back Trick and Treating around the neighbourhood on Halloween… it's far less scary than venturing into this place!

He started tapping his foot and breathing out of his nose.

I rolled my eyes. "Fine!" I said. "But if anything jumps out at me, I'm running for the hills!"

Leah laughed. "That's the Ghost Train!" She laughed some more, then ran inside with John, laughing as they went.

"Yeah, and I'm not going in there either!"

Danny groaned and pulled me again. I took the final few steps towards the curtain. But just before I could disappear into the darkness, the old woman grabbed me around the wrist as she manically shook her head from side to side. What the hell! Surely they're not allowed to touch us?

"Hey!" I said, yelping in fright.

Danny grabbed the woman's hand and pushed her away. "Leave her alone," he said, scowling. She gave an audible sigh and slumped down in her chair again.

My wrist felt like it burned where she'd touched me. She looked scared. Danny took my other hand and pulled me into his hulking chest, thick arms wrapped around me, then he kissed me on my forehead. "Come on, let's catch up with the others."

I nodded, ducking under the thick curtain he held up for me.

As the curtain fell and the lights of reality dwindled away, we became caged in complete darkness.

I stood still, unsure where to move, or even whether to move. How were we supposed to know what to do here? It was much of a show!

The hissing of smoke dwindled around me, and as my eyes started to become used to the black, I could make out slight shapes and forms scattered about. Danny pulled out his phone, putting the torch on, making the mist appear like a wall before us.

The room was enveloped in shadows, with clutter littering the far corner. Old boxes and what looked like a butcher's chopping block had been left there; its surface stained with god only knows what.

The air was heavy and stale, filled with the scent of cinder and mildew. I could hear the scuttling of little feet in the corners. The thought of rats freaked me out more than the vile butcher's block. I hated the bloody things, had done ever since my brother had one that he said would eat through my skin and devour me while I slept. I was six. He was an asshole.

As we moved cautiously into the space, the

warped floorboards creaked and groaned under our feet. I jumped as a rat darted across the floor, disappearing into a hole in the crumbling brick wall. Danny's hand found mine again, gripping it tightly.

"Can we just go?" I almost yelled. He laughed.

"You're fine. You've got me to protect you."

I feigned a smile. I'm not feeling very protected right now, that's for sure!

Taking a few deep breaths, I followed Danny as he walked over to the butcher's block, waving about a rusty meat cleaver around like some demented fool. It was times like this that I contemplated my life choices.

Pulling out my own phone, I checked. No missed called from Leah, so they must have carried on through. My battery beeped. Damn it! Bloody charger never works! Another issue I have with rats, they eat chargers.

Heading over to Danny, I stepped into the

light. Its reassurance bathed me.

"So, what now?" I whispered. All I could hear was our shallow breathing and the drumming of my heartbeat in my ears. This room felt all kinds of wrong, dangerous even. Especially with my idiot boyfriend wielding a butcher's knife around in the dark! I wanted nothing more than to turn and run back out into the light. But some morbid curiosity kept me rooted there with Danny in the shadows.

Danny shone the torch all around the room, covering all four walls until a dark figure ran through the torchlight. I screamed and grabbed at Danny's arm. "Shit!" He yelled. "Don't come any closer… I've got a knife and know how to use it."

I gripped his arm tighter. That freaked me the hell out… I almost laughed. This whole place was meant to be freaky, right? It was all part of the show.

Danny swung the phone torch around back and forth like a crazy person until he swung it too far and it shot out of his hand, clattering in the other corner of the room, a beacon of light shining upwards. "FUCK!" he yelled, waving his hands back and forth with the knife stretched out in front of him as he made his way to pick it up.

As the warmth of his body left me, my nerves kicked in again. There's someone else in here with us. There's rats in here with us. In the pitch black. My heart raced like a train veering off of its tracks. Rats that eat you from the inside out. I whimpered.

"Got it!" Danny said. I could hear the relief in his voice. But when he picked it up, and shone the torch at me, he stilled, a shaky hand pointing at me. "It's…" I frowned. "It's behind you…"

My eyes widened, mouth dried up, and I stood frozen to the spot, eyes darting left and right, looking for a weapon. But there was nothing in reach, just a dirt filled floor, and a stained butcher's block that looked like it was nailed down.

I gulped, fists pummelled, ready for the fight of my life, all while my idiot hulk of a boyfriend looked like he was going to piss his pants. Slowly turning around, I came face to face with a beast of a man, hooded, and looking down so I couldn't see his face. Backing up away from him, I heard him whisper in his deep authoritarian voice, "Mollykins is such a nice name."

His head started to raise, and with Danny's shaky torchlight I could see his mouth as it elongated past his lips, sliced open, up and into his cheekbones. He reminded me of a sadistic Joker character, his face still bloody from something, with black make up blasted around his eyes. His whole appearance perfected for the Freak Show.

He stepped toward me. "Back up!" I shouted at him. His slithering grin stirred a deep well of fear in my soul.

"Now now Mollykins," he purred, a voice laced with darkness. "Let's get you seated for the show, shall we…" he grinned again. This didn't seem right. None of this seemed like a show to me. Where were the rest of the audience? Where were my friends?

His thick hands reached out towards me, tipped with nails that looked more like claws. I stumbled backward, but he was surprisingly quick for his size, closing the gap between us in an instant.

"Danny!" I screamed, hoping he'd regained his senses enough to help me. When I glanced back, Danny was pale, rooted to the spot with fear, but he managed to lift the knife in a feeble attempt to defend us.

The hooded figure chuckled, a low, menacing sound that echoed off the grimy walls of the room. "The only way out is forward," he howled with laughter, his hood falling off, revealing his bald head with a crown of bones sewn into his skin. What the actual fuck! I stood, horrified. He looked like a sadistic prince of darkness. That had better be make-up!

He turned his gaze back to me, his smile widening further as if it would split his face. "Come on Mollykins, I can show you the way forward," He stepped towards us.

"Get back," Danny yelled, giving me the torch as he swung the cleaver around wildly.

I needed a plan... fast. We need to get the hell out of here. I looked to the side where the curtain was. But there was now a door bolted over the entrance. He'd locked us in here. Shit! Looking around, I saw slithers of light from beneath the wall to the right-hand side of the room. A secret door... it must be.

With no weapon within reach and Danny barely keeping it together, options were slim. I looked around frantically. The butcher's block. The nails might be old and rusty... perhaps I could pry it loose.

As the crowned prince advanced, I feigned defeat, dropping my guard and slumping my shoulders as if resigned to my fate. His confidence swelled, and he slowed, savouring his presumed victory. That's when I made my move.

With all the force I could muster, I dashed towards the butcher's block and threw my weight against it. It groaned under the pressure, but didn't budge. Desperate, I kicked at it wildly until finally one nail gave way just enough for it to tilt.

He paused, intrigued by my sudden burst of activity. Taking advantage of his momentary distraction, I ripped a large chunk of wood from the block.

Armed now with a makeshift club, I swung it with all my might as he approached again. The wood connected with a thud against his temple, staggering him momentarily. This was our chance.

"Danny! Run!" I yelled, grabbing his arm and pulling him towards the door we had entered through. The figure recovered quickly; his groan turned into a roar of anger as he charged after us.

I bolted toward the secret door, slammed into it, and light flooded the room. Danny jumped through behind me, slamming the door shut. My breath was loud in my ears while behind us the haunting laughter of our crowned prince echoed, blending horrifically with the creaks and moans of the fucked up Freak Show.

"We need to find another way out," I gasped as we ran, dodging debris and cobwebs that festooned the corridor. Danny nodded silently beside me, both of us aware that escaping this nightmare was all that mattered now.

2

My mind was slammed up against the brink of reality and insanity. Had I just witnessed a guy that seriously slit their mouth like that... for what? Fun? The same psycho that implanted someone's bones on to their skull... I shuddered. Whose bones were they? They looked small enough to be from fingers. Is that what's coming next? A fingerless man?

Trying to get out of my head, I turned to Danny. For a tanned football star, he looked pale and weak right now. My heart was still pounding in my chest, threatening to burst out of me at any second. The flickering lights of the narrow corridor struggled to pierce the oppressive darkness. Every shadow seemed a monster; every sound, a threat. The dank hallway branched ahead, offering two paths.

We had stopped to catch our breath, keeping an eye on the way we came from in case the smiling prince was hot on our heels. But this place was a labyrinth. It felt like we kept going round in circles with no way out. Except one. I gulped, looking ahead at the doors.

"Are you okay Mollykins?" I shuddered at the name. He came over and curled a piece of my brown hair behind my ear.

I nodded. "Shouldn't I be asking you that?" My eyes narrowed. "What happened in there?" I had discovered more than one thing tonight, and the one that bothered me the most was that my boyfriend was a coward.

He sighed, lowering his head. "I... I don't know. I just froze up, I guess." He shrugged, kicking at the dirt on the floor.

"Well, your freeze up could have cost me my life!" I was pissed. It was his idea to come into this damn place. He had been the ever-sweet boyfriend, saying all the right things, then bang as soon as shit hit the fan, he was nowhere to be seen. Asshole.

"I know, and I'm sorry Mollykins."

I growled. "You don't get to call me that anymore!"

He stepped forward, pulling me into his arms as a tear careened its way down my cheek. I tried to push him back, but he wouldn't let me, allowing me to gently sob in his arms.

"I am sorry I wasn't there for you. It's just..." He turned away from me, looking at the floor. "I get nightmares." I looked up at him, wiping my eyes and sniffling.

"What do you mean?"

"Well, my dad has always said, FACE YOUR FEARS SON! so I thought why not... maybe he's right."

Stepping back, I looked at him, brow furrowed. "What aren't you telling me?"

"It's this place…"

"Yes?" I crossed my arms.

"It's given me the creeps since I came in here as a kid. Something happened here. I don't know what, but… well, I get nightmares."

"What kind of nightmares?"

He shuddered as if he was picturing them. "Faces of freakish people. Their mouths are always too big or eyes too wide. Some of them even have clothes made of… well, people."

"What!" I half-yelled. Then realised it sounded like way too close to Hannibal Lecter for me.

"By any chance did you watch Silence of the Lambs as a child?"

He shook his head. "Never seen it. My psychiatrist advised against it."

"Psychiatrist?"

"Yeah, the parents got me help when I was eight. They said I shut down after coming to the Carnival."

"So they think something happened to you here?"

"They don't know, but the police investigated the whole thing. It was when that girl from class... what was her name... the one that went missing?"

"Clary I think,."

"Well, it happened at the same time. The police thought I might have seen something."

"What about your parents?"

"Well, you know what they're like!" I nodded. His parents weren't going to win any parenting awards anytime soon. I doubt they even knew Danny was here right now. Shit. I gulped. With my parents away too... there was no-one that would come searching for us.

"What do you think happened?"

"I just remember a cage with a woman and a wheel she used to turn. It pulled the intestines right out of her body, twisting them around the wheel." I gasped.

"Thus, the psychiatrist."

He shrugged.

"I know something happened. I just can't remember what. So, I had to come back here... had to find out."

"I hope to god you're wrong, Danny. Because if what you saw is true... we've got to get out of this place like yesterday."

As we walked along, I swatted him on the arm.

"Hey! What was that for?"

"You bought me into this shitty place knowing that, asshole!"

He sighed. "Good point! I just hoped it was all in my head, and I knew I wouldn't be able to do it without you there with me." I smiled, but swatted him again.

"Who would have thought the star of the football team needed a girl to hold his hand?"

He laughed, pushing me aside. "I happen to quite like holding your hand."

Hand in hand, we continued down the corridor, trying all the doors, but they were locked. The corridor twisted oddly, distorting perspectives as if the very walls conspired to confuse and disorient us. Old portraits lined the mouldy wallpaper, their eyes seeming to follow our desperate attempt to escape.

As we pushed forward, the air grew colder, prickling our skin with ghostly fingers. A faint melody drifted through the air—an eerie lullaby that seemed to seep out from the very walls. It was hypnotic, almost enticing us to slow our pace and succumb to the weariness that clawed at our muscles.

Danny looked at me, his face paled.

"Do you remember the music?" I asked. He nodded. Shit.

Hands clammy, breathing faster, I pulled Danny by the arm when he slowed. "We have to keep moving," I said. Just then, one door opened. I paused, held Danny's hand tighter, and we stepped into a vast room that was horrifyingly decorated as a scene straight from a nightmarish fairy tale.

It was grotesquely set up like a portrayal of Red Riding Hood, but with a macabre twist.

The theatrical scene portrayed an old stone house with a large fireplace that crackled ominously at one end of the room, casting eerie shadows over the figures in the centre. A pot hung over the fire, with a wooden rail of clothes in front drying. Beside that there was an old armchair, and a light coloured rug that changed colour like a chameleon against a blood red body.

My stomach churned as my eyes adjusted to the horrific sight...Leah. My best friend since diapers was wearing a red hooded cloak, and lying motionless on the floor. Her chest barely moved beneath the deep crimson that soaked through her clothing and pooled onto the rug and floorboards below. Above her hovered a figure so monstrous it could only have been plucked from a nightmare; a man, large and imposing, dressed in the tattered guise of a wolf, his face obscured by an elaborate mask. But the most chilling detail was undeniable–this wolf-man was not merely hovering; he was feasting.

Danny gasped beside me, his voice a whisper of disbelief. "Leah..."

Frozen in horror, I clutched Danny's arm tighter. Leah's arm twitched weakly towards us; her fingers stained red and shaking. The 'wolf' let out a guttural growl, saliva dripping from his mouth like rabid foam.

"This isn't real," Danny whispered hoarsely beside me... but Leah's feeble movement proved otherwise.

My eyes widened while a million thoughts screamed through my mind. The wolf-man had me in his sights now, and unless I moved. I would be the next body he disembowelled.

Gripping another piece of timber from a broken chair nearby with trembling hands, I steeled myself as the 'wolf' crouched low, preparing to charge. "We need to help her," I muttered, though my voice seemed detached and distant in my ears.

As he leapt towards me with unholy speed, eyes wild with fury and madness, I swung with all my remaining strength. The wood connected once again with a sickening crack against his skull. He stumbled but didn't fall, instead regaining balance unnervingly quick.

"Danny! Get Leah! Now!" I cried out.

Danny rushed to Leah's side, trying to staunch the bleeding while I kept myself between them and this monstrous parody of a wolf-man. Leah's eyes fluttered as she tried focusing on us; pain and confusion warring in her gaze.

I could hear more footsteps now. Others were coming. Whether they were friend or foe, I couldn't tell. But their heavy, hurried pacing, along with furious shouts, grew louder in the distance. Desperation gripped me tighter than ever; we couldn't be cornered like this.

"Help is coming," I reassured Leah, trying also to convince myself as her breathing grew shallow and erratic under Danny's makeshift bandage of torn fabric from her own shirt. The fabric was dyed red now, a stark contrast to its once vibrant pink.

The wolf man growled, shaking its head as it launched forward and landed on top of me. I screamed, holding its jaw away from my neck, jolting side to side, thrashing about trying to get it off of me. It snarled, biting again and again, trying to reach my skin. My arms began to shake. It would be mere moments before my strength waned. I cried out just before it did, turned to the side, its jaw snapping at my neck but missing it. Then, when it rose back up, I knew this was it. My eyes widened. I held my breath and waited for the bite that never came. Instead, the wolf man slumped down on top of me, knocked out cold. Above him was my victorious boyfriend, Danny.

He held out his hand, pushing the wolf off of me, and pulling me up into his arms.

Tears streamed down my face, and he held me tight to stop me from shaking. "It's okay now, shhhh, you're okay now," he soothed, stroking my hair until my body calmed and fear settled down to a more manageable level.

"Come on, we need to get Leah out of here," he said. "I don't know how long she has."

The sounds of running footsteps echoed through the corridor. Whoever these people were, they were close.

Danny scooped Leah into his arms with surprising gentleness for his rugged appearance. He nodded at me, his expression set in a grim line of determination. "Lead the way, Mollykins. I've got her." I nodded and smiled at him, broken inside at how my best friend Leah looked.

Turning hastily, my boots slipping slightly on the blood as I guided us through the scene to an open door at the back of it. Keep going forward, I thought. That's what the creepy smiling Prince said.

The echo of our pursuers bounced off the walls, creating a disorientating sound that seemed to come from every direction.

As we turned a sharp corner, Danny kicked a door open, and we spilled into another hallway. It was narrower this time and cluttered with debris. It looked like it hadn't seen visitors in decades. The air was musty, thick with dust and decay.

He slammed the door shut, throwing his weight against it. The wood creaked under his force. Scanning the room quickly, I spotted a large metal filing cabinet and dragged it over with all my might as it screeched in defiance. Danny placed Leah down and helped me as we barricaded the door, positioning it under the handle barricading the door. I half smiled. That should hold for a little while, at least.

Turning around, I found Leah lying down

gently against the wall. Her face was ghostly pale now, her lips tinged with blue. I knelt beside her, pulling off my jacket and wrapping it around her trembling form. "Hang in there," I whispered, pressing her hand between mine as Danny worked to tighten the bandage around her wound.

She managed a weak smile that didn't quite reach her eyes. "Never thought I'd get to see you play hero," she rasped jokingly.

I smirked. "I have you know I was an excellent Wonder Woman for Halloween last year!" She laughed, choking up blood as she did so.

"Do you remember…" she half said, half gurgled. I nodded, holding her hand tighter. "Remember what Danny and John wore," she tried to laugh. I laughed with her. They had come as salt and pepper bottles. But instead they looked like walking dicks.

"What?" Danny said, brow furrowed.

"She means you both looked like walking dicks."

He gasped, hand to his heart. "I am truly distraught right now," he said, laughing.

Leah choked on her laughter again. "I will miss it all," she said, eyes waning.

"What! No!" I grabbed her chin, looking into her eyes. "Stay awake!"

Her head lolled against Danny's shoulder; her face pale as moonlight against his dark jacket. "I'm so cold," she whispered faintly.

"Stay with us, Leah." Danny's voice broke slightly as he adjusted his grip around her, removing his jacket and placing it over her shoulders.

Just then, the sound of thudding against our barricaded door sent a fresh wave of fear through me. They were catching up.

"We can't stay here," Danny said urgently as he scanned the corridor for other exits. It was sparse, aside from some old pipes running along the ceiling and what appeared to be another door further down.

"We've got to go forward," I said, remembering what the smiling creep whispered.

Danny nodded and carefully picked Leah up.

"Stay with us Leah, we're almost there!"

"John," she said, gurgling. That's a good point. Where is John?

"Where is he?" Danny asked, as we continued walking fast towards the other door.

"He left me..." Tears flecked her sorrowful expression, snow white skin kissed by blood. She was broken inside and out, and her love had left her to be mauled by a wolf man, never looking back, never even trying to save her.

"What an asshole!" I said, raising my voice, hands pummelled.

Danny growled under his breath. "We will find him, don't you worry!"

3

As we reached the door at the end of the corridor, I felt a chill creep up my spine. Danny turned the handle slowly, a creak slicing through the surrounding silence. The door swung open with a reluctant groan, revealing a room that looked like a page torn from one of Grimm's Fairytales.

The stale scent of decay wafted from the room beyond, making me want to cover my nose. But I held my breath and followed Danny inside. A solitary bulb hung from a frayed wire in the centre of the ceiling, casting eerie shadows that danced along the walls. Walls that were draped in dark, heavy tapestries that seemed to absorb any light that dared penetrate them.

Beneath the swaying light was a woman at an old-fashioned wooden spinning wheel. Her hair was piled atop of her head in a messy bun, stray silver threads escaping to frame her gaunt face. Her dress was a patchwork of what looked eerily like human skin. Each press of her foot against the pedal of the wheel sent a shiver through the room, performing to the haunting melody that still scratched out of the speakers on the ceiling.

Beneath her, on the cold stone floor, lay John. His eyes were closed, as if in a peaceful slumber, but the gruesome reality was far different. His stomach had been gutted, a sickening display of innards being drawn relentlessly into the spinning wheel. Each turn wrapped more of his intestines into its hungry mechanism.

Danny gasped beside me. "John..." he whispered, horror-stricken. Leah whimpered in his arms.

Darkness flickered over the old woman's vision as the wheel stopped turning and she looked up at us. Her wrinkled skin creased around her lips as she grinned, baring her teeth. "Children," she said, her voice laced with poison as she spat out the words, "why, it is so good to see you."

Mouth agape, I froze on the spot. Danny was physically shaking, backed up against the door we had just come through. This was what he had seen all those years ago. This was the trauma he witnessed. The pain of his young mind having the bear burden to something so tragic made my heart wretch.

The old woman stood up, swaying to the tune as it danced its way around all of us. "Do you like my lullaby, children?" she said, spiting out the words.

I shuddered, and she laughed, continuing her macabre dance towards us. Her steps were unpredictable, jerky movements resembling a disjointed puppet being manipulated by unseen hands. As she drew closer, her eyes sparkled with a feverish gleam that belied her frail appearance.

No matter how fucked up her freakish appearance was. Or the fact she liked to wear human skin as clothing. I was not letting her near my boyfriend or my friend. I stepped forward, placing myself between them and her.

"We need to leave," I said to Danny and Leah, through gritted teeth, trying to keep my voice steady despite the terror clawing at my insides.

The old woman tilted her head back and cackled, the sound slicing through the surreal calm. "Leave?" she crooned, her voice a twisted sing-song. "But, my dear, you've only just arrived."

With a sudden surge of courage, or perhaps desperation, as she neared closer, I demanded, "Tell us how to get out of here!"

The old woman stopped her dance, her eyes

gleaming with a malevolent delight. The woman's smile twisted further, if possible. "Out? Oh, there's always a way out." Her gaze swept over us before settling on Leah with a chilling intensity. "But one of you must stay." She paused dramatically, leaning in so close to me so I could see the myriad of tiny cracks lining her aged lips. "And I choose her." She pointed her scrawny finger at Leah.

Behind me, Danny shuddered, clutching Leah closer. Leah's face was pale, her lips quivering as she stared at the gruesome fate of John. The air thickened with an oscillating fear that seemed almost palpable.

My heart pounded against my chest like a drum, each beat echoing John's dreadful end. Palms clammy, swallowing back bile, I knew. I knew we were stuck here. I couldn't see a way out. There was no door. Nothing.

The walls were adorned with tapestries that depicted scenes as grim as the scene before them… twisted figures entangled in threads of despair, their expressions frozen in silent screams. But one stood out. A pattern in the layout of the tapestries, and a slight draft coming from one wall. What was with this place and its hidden passages?

"No!" I said, pushing the woman back. "You can't have her."

She laughed. "You wait and see Mollykins," she taunted. There's my name again. The name Danny calls me. Had they been watching us all along?

I held the woman back, but she didn't fight or try to push past me. "Get Leah," I ordered Danny. He remained frozen to the spot.

"DANNY!"

"My dear," the woman said. "There is never a need to raise one's voice."

I could have slapped her. But Danny snapped out of it and yelped when he realised how close the woman was to us.

"Pick Leah up. NOW!"

He nodded, and picked Leah up in his arms, but she screamed, coughing out blood.

"Oh, your little Leah doesn't have long, dear. Do you want to say goodbye?"

Tears betrayed me, streaming down my face as I kept the woman at bay.

"It hurts," Leah said.

Danny immediately stopped picking her up and tried to help her walk instead.

Danny looked at me as Leah hung from his arm, unable to take a step. "I need your help, Mollykins!"

I looked at the woman, looked at Leah. Then grabbed Leah's other arm and helped drag her to the tapestries past the spinning wheel and John's dead body.

"She will make a fine edition to my cloak," the woman said, calling after us.

I ignored her, hobbling along, struggling with Leah as we made our way to the wall.

"Can you hold her?" I asked Danny. "I need to find the way out. He nodded.

Feeling along the surface of the wall, my fingers brushed over what felt like a seam in the stonework.

There! A loose stone wiggled under my touch. Heart racing, I pressed on it, feeling it give way slightly under the pressure. The wall rumbled and groaned, sliding to the side. I almost jumped for joy when I saw the light of another room ahead. Turning, I went to take hold of Leah's arm, but Danny dropped her.

"Danny! What are you…" My words trailed off as I caught sight of the horror in front of me. The once dimly lit room was now drenched in a blinding, pulsating red light that seemed to originate from the next room. Before me lay my best friend Leah, gasping for air as she choked on her own blood. Next to her was Danny, my boyfriend, his body convulsing as he fell to his knees with a thud. His eyes were wide with terror, his hands frantically clawing at his neck in a desperate attempt to stop the gushing flow of blood. But it was no use. Every inch of his skin was coated in a thick layer of crimson liquid, each beat of his heart causing more and more blood to spurt out of his severed artery. With one ultimate moment of consciousness, he fell forward onto the floor, his face landing directly in the pool of blood beneath him.

I stood frozen. The scene before me seemed to twist and contort into a grotesque tableau of violence and madness. Danny's chest no longer rose, and as I crawled to him, pulling him on to my lap, I could see his vacant expression and his eyes began to discolour.

The laughter of the woman with the knife echoed around the room, a chilling sound that seemed to come from everywhere at once. She stood menacingly close, her eyes gleaming with a dark, unhinged delight. The knife in her hand dripped with Danny's blood, each drop hitting the floor with a sinister hiss.

The pulsating red light intensified, casting eerie, dancing shadows across the walls. It flickered like the heartbeat of some monstrous creature, syncing with the last few beats of Danny's heart. Outside, the wind howled mournfully, as if mourning the deaths that had invaded this space.

I wanted to run, to escape this nightmare that had wrapped its icy fingers around my throat. Yet my feet felt like they were encased in concrete, unable to move, unable to flee from the terror that unfolded before my eyes.

Leah stopped coughing, her eyes flickering in and out of consciousness. It wouldn't be long before I lost her, too. My heart cried out to wake up. To hope this was all a nightmare of some obnoxious kind. Leah's fingers twitched slightly as she struggled against the inevitable pull of death. Her eyes met mine; they were filled with an indescribable mix of fear, betrayal, and pleading.

She mouthed something silent and desperate, perhaps a call for help or possibly forgiveness for dragging me into this hellish scenario. Her life was slipping away with each shallow, laboured breath.

"Look at them," the woman sneered, gesturing towards Leah and Danny with a maniacal wave of her knife. "Once so full of life, and now nothing more than empty shells because of you."

Her words cut through me sharper than any blade. Guilt, shock, and fear knotted together tightly in my stomach. How had things come to this? Only hours before, we had all been laughing together, enjoying what was supposed to be a fun night out. Now, I was watching my world collapse into chaos and violence.

With cold precision, she bent down, pulled Leah closer to her chest in a mockery of an embrace, then plunged the knife into Leah's heart. The sound of tearing flesh was sickeningly audible. Leah's cry was short-lived; it was a hollow sound that seemed to mark the end of her struggle.

I gasped in horror as Leah's body went limp in the woman's arms. The murderer looked up at me again, her eyes gleaming with a dark delight. "And now... you're all alone," she whispered creepily. I kissed Danny on the forehead, laid him down to rest, and stood up. As I knew, it was my turn next.

Backing away slowly at first, I made it into the corridor with the red flashing light. Then when I was free of the room, I sprinted to the end, fumbling for the handle, but my hands were clammy and bloody, slipping off of the metal knob. Tears streamed down my face uncontrollably, making it hard to see.

"Mollykins, are you ready for your grand finale?" I heard the woman cackle, as she gained closer.

Finally wrenching the door open, I stumbled

out into another room, closing the door and barring it shut with the key that was thankfully sitting there in the lock.

4

I leaned back against the door, panting, the cold sweat mixing with my tears. I was alone. Broken and alone. I wanted to scream, cry, claw my skin off. Anything to take the gut-wrenching pain I felt inside. Heat consumed my body as the anguish filled me, spilling out with nowhere to go but through my tears. Shaking through the agony of losing them, I curled up into a ball on the floor, not caring to look around the room. Not concerned with my own fate. The thought of ending this torment inside bled through me, eased me almost... almost enough to open the door and let the monster in.

"Shhhh!" a timid voice whispered. "They'll hear you!"

I stopped breathing. Tried to control my quivering lip and sobbing heart. "Who... Who's there?" I asked staring through blurred vision from all the tears.

The room I'd entered was dimly lit by a flickering bulb hanging from the ceiling, casting eerie shadows that danced on the damp walls. My heart thundered in my chest as I tried to steady my breathing, listening for any signs of movement from within the room. Where did the voice come from?

"Who are you?" I asked, gaining more control of myself.

As my eyes adjusted to the dim light, I took in my surroundings. The room was long and narrow, reminiscent of a cage lined with rusted iron bars that stretched from floor to ceiling. But with a cage door on the other side that sat ajar.

The concrete floor was covered in grime and scattered debris. Along one wall were stacks of filthy cloth scraps and broken tools. A pervasive smell of mould and decay hung in the air, making it difficult to breathe.

At the far end of the room, I noticed movement. My eyes widened as I saw a girl about my age, her figure slight and bent under the weight of heavy chains that wrapped around her wrists and ankles. She was dressed in tattered rags that barely shielded her from the chill in the air, her hair matted and unkempt. Desperately, she scrubbed at a stain on the floor with a frayed brush.

Hesitantly, I approached her, my steps echoing softly in the chilly space. "Hey," I whispered, not wanting to startle her too much. She looked up sharply, fear evident in her wide eyes as they met mine. Quickly wiping away tears with the back of her hand, she pressed a finger to her lips.

"Shh! Please... they might hear," she murmured anxiously.

This girl looked about as broken as I was. Is

this what they do to the survivors here? Chain them up and make them clean up their mess? I almost shook my head in disgust. My hands balled into fists and my anger rose to the surface. I swallowed it down, for the girls' sake.

So I didn't appear as threatening. I knelt down beside her and gently placed my hand on her skinny arm. "I won't let them hurt you," I promised quietly. "What is this place?"

Her eyes darted around nervously before she leaned closer. "This," she replied in a voice barely above a murmur, "is where the ugly sisters work." The way she said 'ugly sisters' might have been metaphorical—people so cruel that their nastiness seeped into their very nature.

"I'm called Jess, but call me Cinders," she continued, her voice quivering.

I frowned, confusion knotting my brow as I glanced around at our grim surroundings. "Why the name Cinders?"

She shrugged slightly, a hint of bitterness

creeping into her voice. "Because to them, I'm nothing but ashes… worthless and forgotten." Her chains clinked softly as she moved slightly closer to me. "But I believe, one day, I will rise from the ashes and burn the whole place down." She smiled. I smiled back, deciding there and then she was my kind of friend.

"Well, how about we turn that dream into a reality?"

Cinders almost grinned and nodded, then looked around the room, shaking her head sadly. "It's no use; there's no escaping them," she said resignedly.

I reached out, taking her hands gently in mine despite the cold metal that bit into her skin. "We can try together," I insisted. Somehow, I knew leaving without Cinders wasn't an option, not when fate had led me here.

At that moment, footsteps echoed from the direction of the door through which I had entered. My breath hitched in my throat; icy fear gripped me once more. Cinders shrank back into herself.

I swiftly looked around for anything that could assist in opening her cage or defending ourselves but found little more than broken pieces of metal and wood—remnants of what once might have been other furniture or tools.

The footsteps grew louder and then paused by the door I had locked shut—the only thing keeping us separated from what horror lay outside, wanting to get in.

"Mollykins," came the hauntingly familiar cackle from behind the door.

Frantically, I pulled at Cinder's chains. "Where's the key?" I yelled, too afraid now to give a shit about any ugly sisters. We needed to get the heck out of here! Cinder's face paled as she stood up, her legs wobbling. She was skeletal. They'd barely fed her. How the heck she had any energy to scrub that floor, I have no idea. Her shaking arm rose, lifting the heavy chain as she pointed to the other side of the caged room, beside the door that stood ajar.

"There," she said. "They always left the key just out of reach."

I growled under my breath and ran for the hook, slipping on the wet suds mixed with age old blood stains that Cinders had been clearly scrubbing away.

"Mollykins... I hear you in there. Have you found a friend?" The old woman yelled from behind the door.

I choked back a cry, grabbing the key from the metal hook and running back to Cinders.

The door banged. The woman was hammering her fists against it now, humming that creepy lullaby that freaked Danny out and will forever stay etched in my mind. Danny... my heart wept at his terrified face as he realised his demons were real.

"Quick," I yelled. Cinders held out the first of four locks. The key worked, unlocking her right hand. We hurried to her left, then onto her ankles. She rubbed her wrists. They were so red and sore that dry skin flaked away as she cried out at how much they hurt when she touched them. But the relief she must have felt was worth the pain as she kept on doing it.

Eventually, she was free. Unchained and standing up, yet wobbly and faint… but free. This girl needed food and water. She had better not pass out on me. I checked my pockets, but all I had was a pack of chewing gum and Danny's favourite chocolate bar. I always kept one spare, as his sugars crashed late at night.

"Here," I offered it to her. Her eyes widened, and her mouth salivated.

"Are you… are you sure?" She acted like it was a diamond necklace or something.

"Yes, wolf it down. We need to go and I can't have you passing out on me."

"She nodded, savouring the first bite." I smiled, watching her. She reminded me of my baby cousin's first bite of chocolate when Aunt Jane weaned him from milk and he stole her chocolate bar from the table. His face was a picture.

As she took the second bite of the chocolate, the foil wrapper crinkled softly in her trembling hands. Her energy seemed to flicker back like a weak flame rekindled by a passing breeze. I could see a bit of colour returning to her cheeks, each bite appearing to infuse her with life.

"Better?" I asked, and she nodded again, this time with a small smile.

"We need to keep moving," I urged gently, knowing the dangers were far from over.

Together, we stepped cautiously through the slightly open door, which creaked on its hinges as if protesting our escape. I closed it and pulled down the metal bar, locking it from the inside.

What lay beyond was a room that seemed yanked from the pages of a derelict fairy tale. The fireplace crackled, casting long shadows on the walls. A wooden table sat in the middle of the room, surrounded by four rickety chairs that seemed to groan under their own weight. But under the light of the fire that lit the room, three circular shadows sat before the chairs.

"No," Cinders said, grabbing my arm. "You don't need to see them. The concern was etched into the lines on her brow, the narrowing of her eyes, the pursing of her lips. Something about this picture was wrong. Very wrong.

"Them?" I asked, pulling free from her grasp and edging towards the table as shadows danced eerily above it.

I heard Cinders audibly gulp. Her arms were wrapped tight around her body, head lowered. What wasn't she telling me? She knew this place. She'd seen it a thousand times over. So why was she so afraid?

As I reached the table, the fire gleamed and glared, ravaging the logs in the fireplace, lighting up my surroundings and allowing my eye to see first-hand what lay before me on the table.

Three out of four of the plates were filled. Each was covered in blood, guts, and a macabre dish to delight any cannibal. But the round circular centrepiece of each large plate was a human head, their eyes closed as if in an eternal slumber. Danny's familiar features, Leah's sweet face, and John's stern look were eerily preserved on the cold porcelain.

I gasped, my hand flying to my mouth in horror, as I stumbled backwards into Cinders, body trembling. "This can't be real," I whispered, tears brimming my eyes.

Bile wretched up and out of my throat, scolding me from the inside out as I cried out in pain at how these monsters had butchered my friends.

Cinders grabbed me, gripping my shoulders, trying to muster courage for both of us. "We need to keep moving," she urged, looking around at the door we had come through. "This is what they want… to scare us, weaken us."

As we stood there, engulfed in the horror of our discovery, a soft murmur came from behind the door. "Mollykins… shush now, my sweet girl. We saved a plate for you…"

I cried harder.

Was this nightmare ever going to end? Were we ever going to leave this godforsaken place?

Cinders' grip tightened on my arm, her eyes scanning the shadowy corners of the dimly lit room, desperate to find a route of escape. "We can't stay here," she hissed, pulling me along as her boots crunched on scattered debris. I could barely see through my tears, the images of horror imprinted on my mind like ghastly afterimages.

Allowing Cinders to guide the way, we weaved through a labyrinth of oddities and grotesqueries that made up the backstage of the Freak Show. Each turn revealed more bizarre and unsettling displays: jars filled with unidentifiable creatures suspended in formaldehyde, costumes stitched together from what looked horribly like human skin, and old, faded posters boasting the most gruesome acts.

The air was thick with the smell of decay and something metallic I dreaded to identify. Cinders ducked behind a tattered velvet curtain and I followed. Her hands were firm and sure, but I could feel her pulse racing as much as mine.

Suddenly, there was a rustling sound from above. We froze, our breaths held captive in our chests. A shadow flitted across the ceiling – large, imposing, yet swift in its movement. My heart raced, fearing one of the sisters had found us. But no shriek followed, no heavy footfalls - just silence returning like a thick blanket.

"Quick, through here," Cinders whispered, ushering me toward a small service door barely visible under layers of dust and cobwebs. It creaked ominously as she pushed it open, revealing a narrow passageway dimly lit by flickering bulbs that hung precariously from exposed wiring.

The corridor was claustrophobic, lined with peeling wallpaper and embellished with the thrown-away bones of forgotten victims. This was their graveyard. The place where they discarded their victims. I shuddered at the thought of my friend's headless bodies spending an eternity down here. Each step forward felt like wading through syrup, my legs heavy with dread but spurred on with my desperate need to survive and tear down every last building in this godforsaken place.

Cinders paused at a crossroads, listening intently. "We're not far from the back exit," she murmured. "Just past the old animal pens." Her voice was calm but carried an urgency that kept me moving despite every instinct screaming at me to collapse in despair.

As we approached the exit, a low growl echoed down the corridor behind us.

"Run!" Cinders shouted, pulling me forward

with renewed strength. I glanced back to see three middle-aged butch women, their feet pounding the floor, bloodied butchers aprons, and thick round faces filled with anger, as their hungry cries filled the space with terror.

We burst through the back door just as one of the sisters reached us, her butcher's knife glinting cruelly in the moonlight. The cold air slapped our faces, sobering and sharp as we ran into the night.

5

I'd expected bright, blinding lights. The screams of joyous children on fairground rides. But there was nothing. The fair was closed. We ran straight out into a ghost town of forgotten memories.

"Damn!" Cinders cried, panting for breath. "We'll never escape now!"

"Why? We're already out!"

She slammed the service door shut. "Here, help me with this," she urged. I ran over and helped her move a heavy barrel, placing it in front of the service exit. "That should keep them in there for a while."

"Come on, let's find help." I started walking and saw two men walk past in the distance.

"Hey!" I yelled. Cinders grabbed me and pulled me backwards. I tripped and fell. She placed her hand over my mouth.

"Shush!"

My brow furrowed. What was going on? Those guys could call the police!

"Did you hear something, Roger?" I overheard one man say.

"No Jim, now give me a hand locking up."

After they'd walked by, Cinders let go of my mouth and I gasped for breath. She winced, clearly not realising how tight she had held me.

"Why can't we ask them for help?" I asked, confused.

"Because they'll kill us."

"Huh, but why?"

"Don't you get it?"

"Get what? Surely they would want the serial killers captured?"

"Why would they when they're all in on it?"

I gasped, sinking back against the wall of the

Freak Show. "Well, shit…"

She nodded.

Taking a deep breath, I said, "I know there's more you're not telling me." Something rustled around the corner. "But tell me later. We need to get the hell to get out of this place!"

She nodded. "Come on… I'll take you to my hiding spot."

We walked through the carnival; the deadly silence punctuated only by our footsteps crunching on the gravel path. The moon hung low in the sky, disguising the madness with its soft glow, highlighting the giant Ferris wheel as it stood motionless, bearing witness to the carnival's muted victims below.

As we passed the lifeless carousel, its horses frozen mid-gallop, a chill raced down my spine. The painted eyes of the wooden steeds seemed to follow us, their expressions twisted into silent screams. Cinders grabbed my arm and pulled me forward. "Not much farther," she murmured, as she kept looking over her shoulder, her eyes scanning for any sign of movement in the darkened corners.

Finally, we reached the Ghost Train. It sat in the corner of the fairground, its entrance gaping like the mouth of some giant beast. The sign above flickered sporadically, casting an erratic light that made the words "Dare to Ride" seem like a sinister invitation.

Cinders approached a side panel near the back of the ride and expertly manipulated a hidden latch. A portion of the wall swung open, revealing a narrow passage. She glanced around before ushering me inside. Once we were both through, she closed the panel with a soft click that sounded final.

Inside was her sanctuary. Contrary to what one might expect from an attraction named Ghost Train, this small room was cosy and surprisingly welcoming. A small lantern hung from a hook, provided soft illumination. There were cushions thrown haphazardly on the floor, and posters of old fairground attractions lined the walls, giving it an almost nostalgic feeling.

"This is where you hide out?" I asked in awe.

"Yeah," Cinders replied with a nod. "Nobody knows about this place but me," she confided as she closed the panel, enveloping us in darkness, save for our dim lights. "We can talk here."

I finally had a chance to breathe, feeling momentarily safe in this secret pocket of forgotten horrors. I turned to her with wide eyes.

Settling on one of the cushions, Cinders sat across from me, her eyes serious. "Listen," she began, her voice low and urgent. "The people running this place aren't just involved in a few murders; they enjoy the killing…" She gulped and took a deep breath, wiping her clammy hands on her ragged clothes. "After they murder and skin their victims, the ugly sisters sit at the table and feast on their organs."

"What!" I almost vomited.

"It's not just food to keep the carnival folk going. The burgers they sell, are the ones all the kids eat. They're made from the leftovers."

My heart raced as she detailed how this place served as a front for horrific activities after hours.

"How the hell have they not been caught?" I shook my head, cradling my arms around myself. "All those poor kids slaughtered like cattle. How come no one was looking for them?"

Cinders shrugged. "I can only guess they pick off people from out of town, or loners with nothing to live for."

"But we weren't!" I said. "We had everything to live for! Our parents would have searched for us. They knew where we were. So why did the freaks attack us?"

"I don't know." She pursed her lips, thinking for a moment. "You must have caught their attention somehow... and I'm guessing because you're the last one alive, you're the one they were interested in."

"But why!" I cried out.

"Shhh!" Cinders said, looking around and listening to the silence. Nothing. She sighed. "I'm sorry Molly, but I don't know why they picked you. But someone in there took a liking to you."

I shuddered.

As I absorbed her words, there was a sudden clattering noise outside that made us both freeze—a sound that seemed too loud to be just another night creature stirring in the surrounding woods.

Cinders put her finger to her lips and then slowly crept towards a small crack in the wall through which she could peer outside. I watched her face for any sign as she surveyed our surroundings through her tiny window.

"It's okay. It's a dog by the bins."

I sighed, realising I'd been holding my breath. She smiled.

We sat there in silence for a while,

contemplating what the hell to do now. From what she'd told me, the place was locked up tight until sunrise, which was around six hours away. I hoped we could stay there for that amount of time, maybe get a little sleep, but to be realistic there wasn't any chance I'd be shutting my eyes again!

Cinders shifted her dirty hair behind her ear and I noticed her sore marks on her wrist again. I bit my lower lip, thinking. If she had been chained up, then how did she find this place? How did she know her way around here and why did she never escape? A sinking feeling resided in my gut. Had I been played? Was this all part of some game?

Cinders looked at me, her eyes narrowing.

"What's wrong?" she asked.

I looked around for a weapon, but unless I wanted a pillow fight, there was none.

"How did you find this place if you were chained up all the time?"

She smiled, then took a deep breath.

Gretel.

My eyes narrowed.

"Who?"

"The old woman outside the Freak Show," she would come and release me when the ugly sisters weren't around.

"So why didn't you run?"

"Because I couldn't leave her behind, or my best friend, her daughter Esme.

"Who is this Gretel?"

Cinders smiled. "I don't really know. But the story goes that she was found on the roadside pregnant and cut up badly."

"The ear and eye?"

She nodded. "Yes. Who ever did it removed her tongue too." I gasped, swallowing bile back.

"Who the hell could do such a thing?"

"Well, no-one knows for sure. But after the fair folk found Gretel and tended to her wounds, they found her name sewn into her clothing.

That's when they realised. She was wanted for murder."

"Huh?"

"They saw on the news that a local woman had been beaten to death. She was the treasurer to some church or something."

"Do you think it was her?"

She shrugged. "I don't know. But Gretel is the kindest woman I know... she will do anything to protect her daughter."

"Why didn't she ever leave then?"

"She couldn't. She had to look after her child, and the carnival folk saw her as one of them. They would never hurt her or Esme."

"That's good... I guess. So you can still leave, right?"

She nodded. "Yes," then she sighed. "But I made a promise to Esme that if I could ever escape I'd take her with me."

Taking a long breath, I sighed, slumping down against the cushions. This night suddenly got a lot harder.

Cinders turned away and stared out of the hole. The wind howled, crying out to be noticed. "I see them," Cinders said.

I sat bolt upright.

"The sisters, they're out and looking for us."

"If they find you, what will happen?"

"I think this is it for me. After I tried escaping before they put those heavy chains on me. They said they were gonna get their money's worth, and I was going nowhere."

I frowned. "Moneys worth?"

The words tumbled out of her mouth, each one laced with a pain that cut deep. "I was once a girl with loving parents and a family," she began, her voice trembling with emotion. "But it was all stolen from me when the Payne family kidnapped me. I was one of the lucky ones... I survived when so many other girls didn't." Her eyes filled with tears as she spoke the name of her sisters. "Evie, Natasha, and... little Beth."

My heart clenched at the mention of her youngest sister's name, remembering my own younger sister who passed away many years ago. It was a pain that never left, a sorrow that caged my body in grief with every breath, my heart pulsating while hers rotted in the ground. I sighed, lowering my head and digging my nails into my palm.

"What happened to them?" I asked.

Her pale lips quivered as she relived the painful memories. "The brothers sold us at an auction after we tried to escape," she said, her voice barely above a whisper. "I believe Evie and Natasha made it out, but little Beth... they gutted her right in front of us." The tears streamed down her face, leaving streaks in the dirt on her cheeks.

"I'm so sorry about your sister," I said sincerely, feeling a lump form in my throat.

She nodded and sniffled, using a dirty hand to brush away her tears and tangled golden hair. "Thank you," she replied softly.

"So the carnival people bought you at auction?" I asked, trying to process everything.

"Yes… well, Aaden did."

I nodded, wondering where this Aaden person was now. "And where is he now?" I asked, hoping for some answers.

"I don't know," she admitted with a shrug. "The ugly sisters had an argument with him and took me away. After that, no one saw him again."

My heart sank at the realisation that Aaden was likely never coming back for her. "So, when was the last time you were free?" I asked, my voice barely above a whisper.

She furrowed her brow as she tried to remember. "I... I remember my eighth birthday at home," she said, a distant look in her eyes. "But after that... it's all a blur."

My jaw dropped at the realisation that she had been held captive for eight, possibly nine years. "Shit..." I cursed under my breath, unable to comprehend the horror she'd endured.

"I know," she sighed, exhaustion evident in her voice. She fell back against a few cushions, trying to find some semblance of comfort.

I yawned, stretching and leaning back.

"If you need to rest, I can keep watch for a few hours," she offered.

An overwhelming sense of guilt washed over me. This girl had been held captive all of that time, was as skinny as a rake, with zero energy, and was now offering to take care of me!

I shook my head. "No, you rest," I insisted. "I'll keep watch. I won't be able to sleep!"

She nodded. "Okay, but if you hear anything, wake me up."

I nodded, and she closed her eyes, finally allowing herself to drift into a restless sleep. I sat there watching over her, wishing there was something I could do to take every ounce of pain she had been through.

6

As I stumbled through the darkness, the room began to twist and contort around me. The walls were now lined with sharp, bloodied skewers that seemed to pulsate with malevolent energy. My eyes widened in horror as I saw the bodies of my loved ones impaled on gruesome spikes. With shaking hands, I reached out, my fingertips trailing across them, jumping back as their icy skin felt rubbery to the touch. My boyfriend, best friend, and her lover lay lifeless beside me, their horrified expressions frozen forever. But what truly haunted me was the sight of my mum and dad skewered like meat on a spit, their limbs twisted at unnatural angles, ready for the carnival folk to cannibalise.

The air was suffocating as the crushing weight of despair seeped into my every pore. Blood dripped rhythmically from the spikes, each droplet echoing across the vastness of the room. Where was I? My heart pounded fiercely against my ribcage, threatening to burst through at any moment. Hands clammy, breathing rapidly, the room began to spin. Not now! It can't happen now! Dancing waves of silver sparkles cast over my vision. My chest heaved, gasping for breath. Panic bellowed out of me. I was in the killer's lair, and with the echo of heavy footsteps closing in, I didn't have long.

I tried to move, run away, hide… anything to escape what I knew was coming. But my feet were stuck to the cold, sticky floor as if the blood of my family had turned into some sort of gruesome adhesive. Whimpers escaped my lips as I strained to look away, close my eyes and pretend this wasn't happening. This couldn't be happening! But my eyes refused to obey. My body was drawn to the morbidly horrific scene. It was then that I noticed the faintest glimmer of movement.

From the shadows, three large figures moved towards me. Their walk was jagged, limbs arched and severe. They moved slowly, deliberately, their butch female forms blurring and shifting as if made of smoke and mist. Their eyes, if they had eyes, were dark voids that pulled at the very essence of my soul. This couldn't be them? The ugly sisters were real. Just normal people and normal people can be beaten.

Gulping, I pulled at my thigh, urging my feet forward, but still, my family's blood stuck me in place. The vile sisters with their bloody butcher aprons, razor-sharp cleavers and thick brutish hands had almost reached me.

"Welcome Mollykins," the largest one said. "We have a plate waiting for you…"

With a sickening grin, she raised the cleaver and swung at me. My eyes widened, and I screamed.

Suddenly, like being thrust abruptly underwater only to surface gasping for air, I awakened. Cinders was shaking me. Her features were etched with fear.

"You were screaming," she whispered urgently. "I couldn't wake you!"

My breath came in ragged gasps as I clutched at her arms, grounding myself in her realness. The warmth of her skin banished the residual cold left by the sister's touch.

"It was just a nightmare," I managed to say between breaths.

Outside of our little hidden room, the laughter of three hulking females sounded.

"Come out, come out, wherever you are…"

Cinders looked nervously around as if expecting the ugly sisters to materialise from the walls themselves.

"We need to leave this place," she insisted with sudden fierceness. "Now."

Though shaken and disoriented, I found it impossible to disagree. They'd discovered us. They had heard my screams and found us. We were on the run... again.

She grasped my hand, pulling me up and toward a concealed door at the back of the room, her fingers cold yet reassuring against my trembling ones. We slipped through just as the heavy footsteps of our pursuers echoed nearer, the floorboards outside creaking under their weight.

The door led us into a narrow corridor shrouded in darkness by tapestries of previous victims, their faces screaming out for release. I shuddered, gripping Cinder's hand tighter. It smelt damp in here, and mould began to form, with rot taking over the edges of some of their works of art. Faces, although silent in petrification, sparkled with the glaze of mould as it grew over, shrouding them with its cloth of warmth.

We emerged into the heart of the Ghost Train, an attraction that had once thrilled and chilled but now stood silent and deserted. The track lay ahead, winding its way through scenes designed to spook and scare. The cars were shaped like small, ornate coffins on wheels, their once-bright paint now peeling and faded under the assault of time.

To our left, a skeletal figure perched atop a treasure chest grinned toothlessly at us, its bony hand frozen mid-wave. To our right, a group of wax witches gathered around a cauldron, their faces contorted in silent cackles. Above us, spectral lights flickered sporadically from fixtures shaped like bat wings and spider webs.

We ran deeper into the bowels of the ride, our footsteps thudding on the metal flooring. Behind us, the clomping steps and coarse laughter of our pursuers grew louder.

"Through here," Cinders whispered, tugging me along as we moved deeper into the ride, the path became more treacherous. Fake fog machines sputtered sporadically, releasing bursts of mist that clung to our clothes and made the ground slippery beneath our feet. The darkness seemed to press in on us from all sides, filled with the echoes of long-ago laughter and screams that sent shivers down my spine.

Suddenly, from around a sharp corner, a ghastly figure lunged at us. It was a giant animated spider, its legs spanning across the corridor. Its eyes were red LEDs that blinked in the dim light as it descended from above. Cinders yelped but didn't stop; she ducked under one of its massive legs, tugging me along.

Beyond the spider lay a series of tunnels intending to disorient and confuse. Mirrors lined the walls here, distorting our reflections into monstrous shapes that twisted and elongated into nightmarish forms. We pushed forward, driven by fear as much as determination.

Further ahead was what looked like an old-fashioned train compartment. The door was ajar, swinging lightly on its hinges as if inviting us in for respite. With no time to think twice, we slipped inside and shut the door behind us, taking a moment to catch our breath.

The compartment was surprisingly intact, with plush red seats dusted over time but still emitting an aura of forgotten luxury. Dim overhead lights flickered, as if struggling against years of neglect. We crouched down below the level of the windows, which were grimy and cracked but intact enough to obscure us from view, and I took a moment to calm my breathing before I broke out into pure panic.

Cinders placed her finger to her mouth as she listened, signalling to be quiet... they were near. Fear crept up my backbone, choking me, as my heart beat so fast it felt like it would burst from my chest at any moment. We could hear the sisters' voices grow louder and then fainter as they continued down another path.

Cinders pressed her ear against the door, listening for any signs that they might double back. I took a deep breath, willing myself to move. Eventually, taking time to explore our temporary haven, looking for anything that might be used as a weapon or tool.

My fingers brushed against something metallic tucked beneath one of the seats —a rusty screwdriver with a solid handle. Not much, but it was better than nothing.

Cinders whispered fiercely from across the compartment, "We can't stay here long; they'll search everywhere, eventually."

Nodding in agreement, I pocketed the screwdriver and motioned for her to follow me to the connecting door at the end of the compartment. We slipped through just as the echoes of footsteps seemed to magnify, bouncing down the narrow hallway towards us. The next compartment was darker. The lights completely relinquished their glow here, leaving us swathed in shadows. This grim cover was a blessing as it cloaked our movements from prying eyes.

We edged along the wall, our hands sliding over peeling wallpaper and exposed wires. The ghostly ambiance of the train seemed to pulse with a spectral life of its own —groaning metal, the distant clangs of loose fittings, each sound a chilling reminder of our precarious situation.

Suddenly, a light flickered on in the compartment we had just vacated. Our hearts froze as we heard voices. "They must be here somewhere," one hissed.

Cinders tugged at my sleeve urgently and pointed towards a small service hatch beneath one of the seats. It looked barely big enough for a person to squeeze through, but it was our only chance. We hurriedly pried it open with the rusty screwdriver, grimacing as the metal screeched under our exertions.

With no time to spare, we dropped into what appeared to be an undercarriage storage area just as footsteps thundered into our previous hiding spot. Dust and cobwebs clung to us as we crawled forward in the cramped space, every sound magnified by our fear.

Emerging from the other side of the train, we found ourselves in a deserted section of the old station platform. Moonlight streamed through cracks in the ceiling, casting ghostly patterns on the ground. That's when I saw them –Esme and her old mother Gretel standing near a derelict ticket booth.

Esme was watching us intently, her gaze penetrating even in the dim light. Her mother, Gretel, motioned with urgency but without sound, lips forming words that vanished into silence. She pointed towards an old lockbox attached to one of the support beams, holding up what remained of an ornate roof structure.

We hurried over, my heart thudding loudly in my chest. Esme grabbed Cinders and pulled her in for the tightest hug she could. Cinders smiled and Gretel wiped away the tears that started streaming down her face. Her worn face wearing years of pain and anguish herself. I hate to think what she had endured to get her daughter to safety.

Esme stepped forward and unlocked the lockbox with a small, intricate key that she withdrew from her jeans pocket. Inside was a bunch of keys. "The key to the gates is on here," she whispered softly, handing it over to me with trembling hands.

As soon as my fingers closed around the cool metal of the key, distant shouts alerted us that our pursuers had discovered our escape route and were close behind. Without hesitation, Esme ushered us back the way they had come, behind the ticket kiosk and through a service hatch, while her mother helped secure it once we were through.

"I'm so glad you're here!" Cinders exclaimed.

Esme smiled and threw her arms around her, pulling her in for a hug. She pulled back, looking her up and down. "Are you okay? Did they hurt you?"

"No, I'm good." Cinders looked at me and smiled. "So this is Molly. She saved me, and unchained me tonight."

Esme's face lit up.

"Technically," I said. "We saved each other!"

Esme grabbed me too, squeezing me tightly. I coughed. "Damn, you've got some muscle on you for a skinny thing!"

She laughed. "You need to be tough to survive living here!"

Gretel nodded and tried to say yes. But without her tongue, it sounded all kinds of wrong. My heart dropped for her.

"Molly, this is my mum Gretel."

Gretel gave such a beaming smile. You could see how proud she was of her daughter.

"I'm sorry for what happened to you Gretel," I said. She nodded, but looked despairing. "But I do hope you killed that woman. It sounds like that's the least she deserved!"

Gretel tried to laugh and patted me on the shoulder.

"So, let's get out of here, shall we!" Esme said, smiling.

7

We slipped through just as we heard voices reaching where we had been seconds ago. Blinding daylight momentarily disorientated me. It was sunrise... thank god! It wouldn't be long before the gates were opened. I could almost taste our freedom!

I took a deep breath. The air felt so fresh here, mixed with scents of popcorn and candy floss, it was a subtle difference to the rotted corpses and thick dust I'd been breathing in for most of the night.

As we made our way across the now deserted fairground, the early morning sun bathed everything in a soft, golden glow, transforming the sinister trauma of the night into slightly less devilish versions of themselves. Shadows stretched long and thin across the deserted paths, swaying slightly as if they too were trying to escape the horrors that had just hours before played out under the cloak of darkness.

The rides stood silent and ghostly in the early morning light, their garish colours faded from years of neglect and exposure. The Ferris wheel, a monstrous skeletal silhouette against the dim light of dawn, creaked hauntingly as a gentle breeze passed through.

Esme kept close to Gretel, supporting her with a firm grip under her arm. Gretel's steps were shaky but determined, fuelled by the prospect of leaving this place behind.

Cinders kept her eyes peeled for any sign of movement. Her eyes darting from side to side, her body stiff and reluctant. When a cat ran past, I thought she was going to have a heartache. To be fair, the kitty made me jump too. I think it's going to take me a lot to deal with everything this night has thrown at me.

"Are you okay?" she asked me. I nodded feebly. But realistically, how could I be? I wanted to shout, scream, cry. But that was for later. Right now, I still had to survive… and we were almost there.

Cinders caught up to Gretel, taking her arm so Esme could let go and stretch. We stopped for a moment behind an old burger van, catching our breath. "It's not far," she said, nodding toward the gate. It felt like miles, but perhaps that was my weary legs screaming against the strain I was putting them through.

Esme came and stood beside me. "How are you holding up?" I half-smiled, but my tearful eyes must have said it all. She nodded and lent in, taking me in her arms. "We will get you out of this Molly. But, I am so sorry your friends didn't make it."

Tears streamed down my face and I sniffled,

pulling back and wiping my tear-stained cheeks. I looked over to see Gretel looking at me, her face was full of sorrow. Biting my lower lip to stop it quivering, I took a deep breath and asked, "who hurt Gretel like that?"

Esme's shoulders sank. "It was before I was born… and because of love some might say."

My brow furrowed. "What do you mean?"

"My mum told me what happened once. She wrote it down… it's the only way to be sure of what she says." Esme dug into her pocket and pulled out a note wrapped in a thin old carrier bag to keep it safe. She handed it to me.

"Esme, my love. I wish I could speak these words to you, as any mother would. I wish I could tell you I love you and let you hear the beauty of my spoken word. But I can't, and I will never be able to.

What happened to me, happened for a reason, and it is something I would endure over and over again just to look at your bright, beaming smile every day of my life. You are my everything darling girl, and I will always protect you.

You have asked what happened to me, and who your father is. I can tell you that your father was a wonderful man, he was a local farmer that helped Mama who held me hostage. He and I fell in love, and when he asked that I marry him, I finally told him the truth of my living situation, and of what Mama really was. He vowed to me he would save me, and release me from my pain. But when he tried to help me escape, Mama was ready, and she buried him under the old oak tree in the back garden.

As payment for falling in love, she said she would punish me. Mama was a religious serial killer, and her payment involved me seeing no evil, hearing no evil, and speaking no evil. Thus, this is what she cut from me, so no man would ever want me.

Your father was a good man. It is only days after his death that I realised I was pregnant, and began to form my escape plan, only to be picked up by the carnival folk here."

The rest of the note had been ripped off. The salty taste of tears cushioned my lips, and I looked up to find Gretel nod once and faintly smile. The utter anguish of pain and anger of how these girls, these women had been treated boiled inside of me. Esme took the note from me, held my hand and said, "it was a long time ago. Even though we've been stuck here, my mum and I have had a good life together."

My hands balled into fists. "It isn't fair!" I almost yelled. Esme's eyes widdened. "She escaped, she hoped for a better life for you, only to be thrown into another bloodthirsty murder fest. What the fuck is with that!" Esme nodded, her face lowering. Gretel hobbled over and grabbed me, pulling me into her frail chest. Her heart was beating at a calming rate, her hand stroked my back and she stood there for a moment, letting me cry for her.

Minutes went by until eventually all my tears had been cried out. Gretel let go, hobbled backwards just enough to see my face. She lifted up my chin and kissed my forehead. "It's okay," she tried to say. The noise she made instead of those simple words crushed my soul, and the tears began again.

Wiping away my tears, she smiled and Esme took her arm, as Cinders walked over. "We are going to give them a chance to live to Molly," Cinders said. "This place has been a prison for all of us for one reason or another."

"I know. I just… it's all been… a lot!"

She nodded, grabbed my arm and pulled me along with her.

We passed by the hall of mirrors, its entrance gaping like an open wound. I glimpsed our distorted reflections as we hurried by… twisted and stretched images that somehow seemed too real in their depiction of our current state: stretched thin by fear yet resilient to our escape. A chill ran down my spine when I thought I saw a figure move inside.

"Mollykins…" taunted a voice that carried over the airwaves. Someone had hooked themselves up to the speaker system and continued to hum that creepy lullaby that the tapestry lady with the spinning wheel hummed. I could almost guarantee it was her. She was screwed up enough to want to play with her food. I shuddered.

"Come on!" Esme said, her eyes wide. "They know we're trying to escape… we need to hurry!"

The scent of popcorn and candy floss grew stronger as we made our way through the main concession area. A fire dwindled, nearly burned out and lacking fuel.

Gretel tried to speed up, but with a limp on her right, and being breathless as she walked fast. She wasn't getting very far fast. She stopped just as the gate loomed in front of us.

"Mollykins…" the tannoy boomed, callous cackles followed. "I'm hungry Mollykins."

The sound of pounding footsteps followed not far behind us. I turned to see the ugly sisters closing in. I looked at the gate far ahead, then looked back at them. We weren't going to make it!

I noticed Gretel taking her daughter's face in her hands. "What mum?" Esme asked. Gretel made a noise and pointed to the gate, then kissed Esme on the forehead, pushing her towards salvation.

"No! No, I won't leave you!"

Gretel made another noise that sounded like the word *Go*. She hobbled forward to push her daughter towards the gate again.

Tears flooded down Esme's face. "No mum, they will kill you for helping us escape."

Gretel smiled. She looked at Cinders and nodded, then looked at Esme. Cinders nodded back, taking Esme by the hand. "We have to go. You mum wants you safe. That's all she's ever wanted."

"But I can't leave her!"

"She is staying to hold them off so we can

get away."

Esme's body shook with tears.

Gretel smiled at her and nodded again, just as the three hulking figures of the ugly sisters appeared from the other side of the carousel.

"Mollykins, we're almost there…" the tannoy boomed. I shuddered.

Cinders pulled at Esme, but she was determined to stay. She looked at me. "Help, we need to get her out of here too. If they catch us, we're all dead!"

"Damn it!" I cried, turning back and grabbing Esme's hand, pulling her with all my might.

"No!" she screamed. "I can't leave her!"

Gretel had already started walking towards the ugly sisters. She picked up one of the large sticks from beside the dying fire, carrying it with her.

Cinders pulled at Esme. "Now Esme! Your mum would be heartbroken if she lost you. We need to go."

Esme watched her mum as she reached the ugly sisters. Cinders pulled her into her arms, turning her away from the battle that began. If you could call three against one a battle. Even the four of us wouldn't be able to take on the ugly sisters. I bit my lip… we can't let Gretel's sacrifice be in vain.

I pulled Esme, and she started moving… walking away from her mum, the one and only person in her life that had sacrificed everything to keep her safe. That woman had been through hell and back.

As we ran to the gate, I noticed the hefty padlock hung open, swaying slightly as if nudging us towards liberty. When we reached it, Cinders held on to Esme. Keeping her looking at the gate. I turned back to see Gretel being beaten by her own stick. The sound of crunching bones made my stomach churn and Esme cried out for her mum, covering her ears. But the one thing Gretel did not do, even to her dying breath, is she never screamed once. She didn't want her daughter to hear her pain as she died, wanting to save her one last time.

The ugly sisters were laughing as she fell to the ground, kicking her in the ribs, the face, the stomach.

My fingers trembled as I pulled at the gate's heavy latch, wincing as it groaned. I pulled Esme through, Cinders followed, closing the gate, locking it behind us. Esme stopped and cried out as she saw her bloodied and battered mum on the ground unmoving.

The ugly sisters made their way to the gate. "Well, well… it looks like you're on the wrong side of the gate," the middle one taunted. I gulped. "Now, where was that key?" one sister asked the other.

"GO!" Cinders yelled, and we ran. Ran through the trees and towards down the road. Tall pines stood guard, cradling the fairground in their arms. We veered off of the path, ensuring we couldn't be followed by any vehicle the carnival folk owned.

Behind us, the carnival faded away. The clamour of spooky laughter and mocking chants dissolving into the morning mist that rose from the ground like a last barrier between us and that haunted night.

We moved deeper into the woodland's embrace where dappled sunlight painted fleeting masterpieces on Esme's face... each ray brushing away some of her despair—and for a moment it felt like we could indeed reclaim what horror had tried to steal from us last night: peace.

8

The forest thinned as we approached the edge of town; the trees giving way to the familiar sights of civilisation. It was a stark contrast to the eerie otherworldliness of the carnival and the protective cocoon of the woods. We stumbled onto the pavement, our shoes scuffing against concrete instead of earth, suddenly aware of our dishevelled appearances in the light of day.

Houses lined the streets, their windows like watchful eyes. People started to take notice—curtains twitching, doors cracking open. Our presence, wrapped in bloodied clothes with faces streaked by tears and dirt, drew concern rather than indifference.

It wasn't long before a police car drove up beside us, its blue lights silent but insistent. A young officer stepped out, his expression a mix of confusion and worry. "Is everything alright here?" he asked, eyeing our bare feet and bloodied complexion.

My face paled and tears started rolling down my cheeks. Cinders tightened her grip on me, her hold the only thing holding me upright anymore.

"Hey… what happened?" he asked, pulling out grey blankets from the boot of his car. Cinders wrapped one around me and shared the other with Esme, who remained deadly silent.

"We need to get out of here," Cinders said, looking around nervously.

He looked around as well. "Sure…" he looked at the crusted blood on my top. "Do any of you need medical assistance?"

Cinders shook her head. "Not right now."

"Okay, well, come on. I'll take you to the station, and we can take your statements there."

She nodded, helping me and Esme as we all got into the car.

He escorted us to the police station—a sturdy brick building nestled between a bakery and a barber shop. Inside, it was warm and brightly lit, a stark departure from the shadowed woods and ghostly carnival. We were given hot cocoa and more blankets, wrapped around our shoulders by kind-faced officers who tried to piece together our story from hesitant whispers and trembling lips.

The warmth of the station seeped into our bones as we sat wrapped in blankets, trying to transform back into a sense of normalcy. One by one, we recounted our tale. The officers scribbled notes that seemed far too neat, far too orderly for such a chaotic story. Each word we spoke reconstructed part of last night's terror, but this time within confines that would not let those fears run rampant.

When my parents arrived, their steps were

heavy with urgency and love. My heart wept as they reached me, holding me tight. My mum's tears soaked into my bloodied shirt, each one carrying a flood of emotions: fear, relief, love – in every salty drop.

Before I left, I turned back to Cinders… the friend who had taken command when panic threatened to overrun us both. I wrapped my arms around her, holding her frail body tight. I wouldn't have survived the night without her.

"Thank you isn't enough," I whispered into her ear.

She pulled back slightly, smiling. "You don't owe me anything." She held me tighter. "All I ask is that you put this behind you. Don't let the trauma of this night ruin your whole life."

I nodded, sniffling. She let go of me and wiped her own tears away.

I turned to Esme. "Thank you, if it wasn't for Gretel…" I said, tears flowing again. She nodded and held me tight.

"Be safe Molly," she said. I smiled.

My mum and dad waited outside for me, watching through the open door, as I said goodbye to the two friends that I knew would be forever etched in my heart.

As I walked toward my parents, my footsteps echoed on the wet pavement. They opened their arms, and familiar scents of lavender and cedarwood enveloping me in an embrace that felt like a fortress against the cruel world.

The car ride home was quiet, filled only with the soft hum of the engine and the occasional swish of tires against the damp road. I leaned my head against the window, watching as the cityscape slowly transformed into the more familiar tree-lined streets of our neighbourhood. My mother kept glancing back at me from the front seat, her eyes filled with a mix of concern and relief.

"We're home, sweetheart," she whispered, as we turned into our driveway. "Why don't you go upstairs and get some rest? I'll make us something to eat."

I nodded, too drained to speak. The familiarity of our house—a quaint two-story with a wildflower garden and a cosy front porch—was a balm to my frayed nerves. I trudged inside, pausing only to kick off my shoes before heading straight for the shower to wash away the blood from last night's horrors.

After I was changed into comfortable pyjamas, I entered my bedroom. My one safe space in the entire world. My room was a sanctuary. The walls were painted a soothing shade of lavender, and gauzy white curtains fluttered gently at the open window, letting in a cool breeze that carried the scent of jasmine from our garden. Plush pillows and a fluffy duvet beckoned invitingly from my bed, which stood like an island of comfort amidst my scattered books and art supplies.

I let out a sigh as I closed the door behind

me, leaning back against it for a moment to let its solidness reassure me. Then, with slow steps, I moved towards my bed, slipping under the covers and curling into a ball. The fabric was cool against my skin, grounding me back to reality... a reality where monsters didn't lurk at every corner.

As exhaustion pulled me under and into a deep sleep, I floated in a haze where the horrors of the night began to recede like tides going out to sea. But this reprieve was short-lived.

I awoke abruptly to darkness... a complete absence of light that for a moment made me doubt whether my eyes were even open. My heart raced; something felt different... an eerie chill settled in the air and my skin prickled with apprehension.

A soft singing filled the room, slow and melodic, a lullaby that seemed both beautiful and haunting in the stillness of the darkness. I knew it from somewhere. The pitch, although delicate, gripped me until it choked me. It sounded like one of those ancient lullabies that mothers sung to soothe their children; only this one twisted strangely mid-tune into something darker. As it grew louder, I could feel my pulse pounding in my ears.

Then suddenly, the mattress moved as though something was sitting on it. But I couldn't see. It was too dark. I wiped my eyes, reaching around for my phone for a torch, but it wasn't there. The mattress moved again and I gasped. I wasn't imagining it.

Shuffling back I stared at the bottom of the bed, until shadow by shadow my eyes began to focus. Shapes formed limbs, attached to the bulk of an adult body all dressed in black and perched at the end of my bed. My eyes widened, breathing stopped dead, mouth agape. What was it? Trailing my eyes over the thing at the end of the bed I came to the head. The light from the moon trickled inside the room, highlighting the shimmering of white finger bones that formed a crown; and as he lifted his head into view, the face that stared back at me was the Prince of Darkness himself, with the sliced smile and bloodied teeth just waiting to take a bite out of me.

He grinned and I held my breath, forcing my body as far back into the headboard as I could. This had to be a nightmare. He shot forward until he was mere inches from my face. His breath smelled of decay. His icy hands swift as they grabbed me, pulling me against him and sniffing me, groaning.

Pulling out a blade, he gripped my neck, angling my jaw, and inserting the blade into my mouth.

With the first ounce of pain, reality came crashing down. This was real. He was here. I screamed. Thrashing my legs to get him off me. He laughed, cackled almost; his grin taking over the lower half of his face as he began to cut. Blood. Pain. Flashes of light as my body threatened to pass out. He continued cutting.

The lullaby grew louder.

The swirling of my room became a haze of blood, tears and sweat as I fought to push him off of me.

"There there Mollykins," he said. "That's one side done."

Forcing the blade over to the over corner of my mouth, he sliced my tongue on the way. I choked back the blood. But as he started to cut again, I could no longer see for the amount of tears that took hold of my vision.

The lullaby grew louder.

My heart thundered against my ribcage. Hands clammy and nails clawing at his arms, yet still he would not stop. He liked the pain. But no matter how slowly he sawed at my lips, or how long it took him to slice into my cheek, I knew my parents would be here any minute to save me. I just had to hold out.

The lullaby grew louder and nails scratched

at my bedroom door.

The man laughed, finishing off. He pulled back, letting go of my head to admire his work. Then continued another centimetre more.

My hands whipped up to my face, feeling the bloodied wounds, the gaping holes, the slits from each corner of my mouth all the way up to my cheekbones. He had turned me into him. Made me smile just like him. Forever grinning. Forever dead inside.

The man moved aside, stood up and turned on the main light as his terrifying face came fully into view. He picked up my desk mirror and brought it over, showing me my face. I closed my eyes. I couldn't see it. Daren't see it.

"Open your eyes Mollykins, you will want to see this…"

I gulped, fearful of what he would do to me if I didn't obey.

Slowly I opened my eyes, and piece by piece, the face of a creature from the depths of hell itself stared back at me. Soulless red eyes, swollen from crying a thousand tears, looked back in horror. Crimson red lips were sliced open in the corners. My cheeks were ripped apart with gaping wounds from which the blood flowed freely. I reached up, touching my face. It was me. But it couldn't be. Not like this. I would forever be branded the Freak from the Freak Show. Never escaping this night.

I cried bloodied tears, my whole body shaking as the man stared at me, pleased with himself. My parents should have come, I thought, crying softly now, broken inside and out. Where were they? Why didn't they help me?

The lullaby stopped.

The door flung open, making me jump. The woman with wild grey hair stood there, shrouded by a cloak made from the faces of her victims. My friends, my boyfriend. But what I saw next made me freeze, mouth agape. In each hand, she held a severed head on a plate. My eyes widened, wishing what I saw was untrue. But the dripping of fresh blood on my wooden floor cut the silence. As the heads she held were the screaming faces of my mum and dad, bloodied, gutted, and decapitated.

The man with the sinister smile came into view in front of me and said,

"Welcome to the Freak Show, Mollykins."

OTHER BOOKS BY ANNALEE

The Resurgence series:

The Heart of the Phoenix

The Rise of the Vampire King

The Fall of the Immortals

The Birth of Darkness

The Fire Wolf Prophecies:

Crimson Bride

Crimson Army

The Shop Series:

Stake Sandwich

The Devil Made Me Do It

Strawberry Daiquiri Desire

The Celestial Rose Series:

Eternal Entity

Eternal Creation

Eternal Devastation

Eternal Ending

Gruesome Fairy Tales:

Gretel

Hansel

Red

Wolf

Cinders

AUTHOR'S NOTE

Thank you for reading Cinders, I hope you enjoyed the story! I always appreciate your feedback and would be grateful if you could leave me a review on Amazon– just a few words make all the difference!

As with all authors, reviews mean the world to me. It keeps me going, helps me strengthen my writing style and helps this story become a success.

CONNECT WITH ANNALEE

Join Annalee on social media. She is regularly posting videos and updates for her next books on TikTok and Facebook.

Join Annalee in her Facebook group:

Annalee Adams Bookworms & Bibliophiles.

Also, subscribe to Annalee's newsletter through her website - for free books, sales, sneak previews and much more.

Subscribe at www.AnnaleeAdams.biz

TikTok: @author_annaleeadams

Website: www.AnnaleeAdams.biz

Email: AuthorAnnaleeAdams@gmail.com

Facebook:

https://www.facebook.com/authorannaleeadams/

ABOUT ANNALEE

Annalee Adams was born in Ashby de la Zouch, England. Annalee spent much of her childhood engrossed in fictional stories. Starting with teenage point horror stories and moving on up to the works of Stephen King and Dean Koontz. However, her all-time favourite book is Lewis Carroll's, Alice in Wonderland.

Annalee lives in the UK with her supportive husband, two fantastic children, little dog, and kitten. She's a lover of long walks on the beach, strong cups of tea and reading a good book by candlelight.

Printed in Dunstable, United Kingdom